A NOTE TO PARENTS

When your children are ready to "step into reading," giving them the right books is as crucial as giving them the right food to eat. **Step into Reading Books** present exciting stories and information reinforced with lively, colorful illustrations that make learning to read fun, satisfying, and worthwhile. They are priced so that acquiring an entire library of them is affordable. And they are beginning readers with a difference—they're written on five levels.

Early Step into Reading Books are designed for brand-new readers, with large type and only one or two lines of very simple text per page. **Step 1 Books** feature the same easy-to-read type as the Early Step into Reading Books, but with more words per page. **Step 2 Books** are both longer and slightly more difficult, while **Step 3 Books** introduce readers to paragraphs and fully developed plot lines. **Step 4 Books** offer exciting nonfiction for the increasingly independent reader.

The grade levels assigned to the five steps—preschool through kindergarten for the Early Books, preschool through grade 1 for Step 1, grades 1 through 3 for Step 2, grades 2 through 3 for Step 3, and grades 2 through 4 for Step 4—are intended only as guides. Some children move through all five steps very rapidly; others climb the steps over a period of several years. Either way, these books will help your child "step into reading" in style!

Copyright © 1999 by Raymond Briggs.
Illustrations by Maggie Downer, based on the book THE SNOWMAN by
Raymond Briggs. All rights reserved under International and Pan-American Copyright
Conventions. Published in the United States by Random House, Inc., New York.

www.randomhouse.com/kids

Library of Congress Cataloging-in-Publication Data
Raymond Briggs's The Snowman /
adapted by Michelle Knudsen ; illustrated by Maggie Downer.
   p.   cm. — (Early step into reading)   SUMMARY: When his snowman comes to life,
a little boy invites him home and in return is taken on a flight above the countryside.
ISBN 0-679-89443-8 (trade). — ISBN 0-679-99443-2 (lib. bdg.)
[1. Snowmen—Fiction.] I. Briggs, Raymond. Snowman.   II. Downer, Maggie, ill.
III. Title. IV. Series. PZ7.K7835Rau 1999 [E]—dc21 99-19328
Printed in the United States of America 10 9 8 7 6 5 4 3 2 1

RANDOM HOUSE, STEP INTO READING, and colophons are registered trademarks and EARLY
STEP INTO READING and colophon are trademarks of Random House, Inc.

Early Step into Reading™

RAYMOND BRIGGS'

The Snowman

adapted by Michelle Knudsen

Random House 🏠 New York

Hooray!
It is
snowing!

James gets dressed.

He runs outside.

He makes a pile of snow.

He makes it
bigger

and

bigger.

He puts a big snowball
on top.

He adds a scarf
and a hat.

He adds an orange
for a nose.

He adds coal
for eyes and buttons.

There!
What a fine snowman!

It is nighttime.

James sneaks downstairs.

He looks out the door.

What does he see?

The snowman is moving!

James invites him in.

The snowman has never
been inside a house.

Hello, cat!

Hello, lamp!

Hello, paper towels!

The snowman
takes James's hand.

They go up, up,
up into the air!

They are flying!

What a wonderful night!

It is morning.

James jumps out of bed.

He runs downstairs.

He runs into the kitchen.

He runs outside.

But the snowman
has gone.